Dear Parent:
Your child's love of reading starts here ...

Every child learns to read in a different way and at his or her own speed. Some go back and forth between reading levels and read favorite books again and again. Others read through each level in order. You can help your young reader improve and become more confident by encouraging his or her own interests and abilities. From books your child reads with you to the first books he or she reads alone, there are I Can Read Books for every stage of reading:

SHARED READING
Basic language, word repetition, and whimsical illustrations, ideal for sharing with your emergent reader

BEGINNING READING
Short sentences, familiar words, and simple concepts for children eager to read on their own

READING WITH HELP
Engaging stories, longer sentences, and language play for developing readers

READING ALONE
Complex plots, challenging vocabulary, and high-interest topics for the independent reader

ADVANCED READING
Short paragraphs, chapters, and exciting themes for the perfect bridge to chapter books

I Can Read Books have introduced children to the joy of reading since 1957. Featuring award-winning authors and illustrators and a fabulous cast of beloved characters, I Can Read Books set the standard for beginning readers.

A lifetime of discovery begins with the magical words **"I Can Read!"**

Visit www.icanread.com for information
on enriching your child's reading experience.

I Can Read Book® is a trademark of HarperCollins Publishers.

Superman: Escape from the Phantom Zone

BATMAN, SUPERMAN, WONDER WOMAN, and all related characters and elements are trademarks of DC Comics © 2011. All rights reserved. Printed in the United States of America. No part of this book may be used or reproduced in any manner whatsoever without written permission except in the case of brief quotations embodied in critical articles and reviews. For information address HarperCollins Children's Books, a division of HarperCollins Publishers, 10 East 53rd Street, New York, NY 10022. www.icanread.com

Library of Congress catalog card number: 2010933668
ISBN 978-0-06-188519-8
Book design by John Sazaklis

13 14 15 16   LP/WOR   10 9 8 7 6 5   ❖   First Edition

SUPERMAN™

Escape from the Phantom Zone

by John Sazaklis
pictures by Steven E. Gordon

SUPERMAN created by Jerry Siegel and Joe Shuster
BATMAN created by Bob Kane
WONDER WOMAN created by William Moulton Marston

HARPER
An Imprint of HarperCollinsPublishers

SUPERMAN

Superman was born on the planet Krypton and sent to Earth. Earth's yellow sun gives Superman many amazing powers.

BATMAN

Batman lives in Gotham City. He is an expert crime fighter with an arsenal of cutting-edge equipment.

WONDER WOMAN

Wonder Woman was born on Paradise Island. She is an Amazon Princess and fierce warrior.

GENERAL ZOD

Zod is a power-hungry madman from Krypton. Superman's father sent Zod to the Phantom Zone for his violent crimes.

NON & URSA

Non and Ursa are Zod's loyal followers. They helped Zod escape from the Phantom Zone once.

THE PHANTOM ZONE

The Phantom Zone is an outer-space prison that holds some of the universe's most dangerous criminals.

Superman is in his secret hideout,

the Fortress of Solitude,

when an alarm goes off.

Superman calls his friends

Batman and Wonder Woman.

"My readings show something dangerous is headed toward Metropolis," Superman says.

"We must work together to stop it."

The heroes meet in Metropolis.

"Everything seems fine," Batman says.

"Are you sure there's a problem?"

"Trust me," Superman replies.

Suddenly, a portal opens in the sky
and three strange people appear.
"We seek the one called Superman!"
the leader yells.

"Do you know them?" Batman asks.

"Yes, they are dangerous criminals

from my home planet,"

Superman says.

"We must protect the city!"

shouts Wonder Woman.

"Be careful," Superman warns.

"Here on Earth, they have

the same special powers that I do!"

"I am General Zod," shouts the leader.

"We have escaped the Phantom Zone,

where your father imprisoned us.

Now we will get our revenge, Superman."

"Once Superman is taken care of,"

Ursa says, "we will rule this silly planet.

Humans will be our pets!"

"Earth is my home now," Superman says.

"And I have sworn to protect it.

You are not welcome here!"

"We will crush you!" General Zod cries.

In a flash, he attacks Superman.

The heroes must help their friend.

Batman charges at Non,

but the villain uses his super-breath

to freeze Batman in his tracks.

Ursa blasts Wonder Woman

with her heat vision.

Wonder Woman blocks the beams

with her magic bracelets.

Superman fears that the battle
will harm innocent people.

General Zod holds Superman in his grip.

"You are no match for us," Zod says.

Superman comes up with a plan
and looks at his friends.

He cannot tell them his idea.

He trusts they will follow his lead.

The Man of Steel breaks free

and takes off into the air.

"Catch me if you can!" he yells.

The three villains chase Superman.

He flies to the Fortress of Solitude.

That is where Superman keeps

the Phantom Zone Projector.

It is a special machine that can send

villains back to the Phantom Zone!

Batman and Wonder Woman

follow close behind

in Wonder Woman's Invisible Jet.

They see Superman and the villains

enter the Fortress of Solitude.

"Superman is distracting them
so we can plan a sneak attack,"
Batman says.

"Let's hurry," Wonder Woman replies.
"Before it's too late!"

Zod is impressed with the Fortress.

"This can be our throne room," he says.

"Look, the Phantom Zone Projector!"

Ursa says, pointing to the machine.

"Let's use it on Superman!"

"First things first," says the general.

"Superman will kneel before Zod!"

The villains combine their heat vision,

forcing Superman to his knees.

The hidden heroes leap into action!
Wonder Woman ties up Non and Ursa
with her magic Lasso of Truth.
"How do we send you back?"
Wonder Woman asks.

The lasso forces the villains
to tell the truth.

"The Phantom Zone Projector," they say.

"It will send us back to prison."

Batman races to turn on the machine.

Zod is distracted by the sneak attack.

"You fools," he yells at Ursa and Non.

"Work together! Do not let them win!"

Superman jumps up and says,

"Game over, General. You lose!"

Then he throws Zod into the machine.

Batman flips the switch.

A laser beam blasts General Zod.

"Curse you, Superman!" Zod cries
as he begins to fade away.

Wonder Woman throws Non and Ursa
into the projector's path.
They follow their leader all the way
back to the Phantom Zone!

"Thank you," Superman says.
"We sure showed Zod and his gang
what teamwork really means!"